W9-BXA-912

Trouble in the Ark

Gerald Rose

THE BODLEY HEAD
London · Sydney · Toronto

All the animals were crowded in the ark. It rained and rained and rained. They became very fed up. It was fly who started the trouble.

He ⚡⚡⚡⚡⚡⚡ mouse

who

squeaked

at rabbit

who

squealed

at rhinoceros

who **snorted** at parrot

who *squawked* at snake

who *hissed* at frog

who **crooked** at donkey

who **brayed**

at cock

who

crowed

at goat

who

at bear

who *growled*

at monkey

who **chattered** at pig

who **grunted** at duck

who **quacked** at dog

who **barked** at cow

who
mooed
at bull

who
bellowed
at owl

who *hooted* at horse

who *neighed* at goose

who **honked**

at hedgehog … who

snuffled

at wolf

who *howled*

at hen

who

cackled

at cat

who *meeeowed* at lion

who *roared* at elephant

Just then dove flew
in with an olive twig.
The rain stopped and
Mrs Noah sighted land.

Noah was delighted and shouted:

Yuhoo! Yippee!

All the animals were
glad to leave the ark,
and Noah and his wife
were left in peace ...

well almost.